HUGGA BUNCH is a trademark of Hallmark Cards Inc., used under license.
HUGGA BUNCH designs © 1985 Hallmark Cards Incorporated. All rights reserved.
Library of Congress Cataloging in Publication Data: Cowell, Phyllis Fair. A Hugga Bunch hello.
SUMMARY: Bridget visits Huggaland and finds a way of keeping her grandmother from going to a nursing home. 1. Childrens' stories, American.
[1. Hugging — Fiction. 2. Grandmother's — Fiction. 3. Family life — Fiction]
I. Lipking, Ronald, ill.   II. Title.
PZ7.C8354Hu   1985   [E]   85-3592   ISBN 0-910313-90-3
Manufactured in the United States of America   1 2 3 4 5 6 7 8 9 0   -01

PROOF OF PURCHASE
A Hugga Bunch Hello.
H.B.

HUGGA BUNCH™

A Hugga Bunch Hello

Story by Phyllis Fair Cowell
Pictures by Ron C. Lipking

Bridget Severson hugged each of her stuffed animal friends. Bridget liked to give hugs. She liked to get them too. But hardly anyone in Bridget's house gave hugs anymore.

Certainly not Andrew, her older brother. He said, "Hugs are gross! Anyway, boys don't hug."

Aunt Ruth was even worse than Andrew. She pushed Bridget away, as if a hug might soil her clothes or muss her hair. Bridget's mother and father *did* like to hug, but lately they were just too busy.

Only Grandma took the time to hug now.
Sometimes Grandma forgot telephone messages or
where she left her glasses. But she never forgot to
give Bridget a hug.

Yesterday, Bridget overheard voices in the living room.

"It's the best place for you," Aunt Ruth was saying to Grandma. "You'll be with people your own age."

"I'll...I'll think about it," Grandma mumbled and wandered slowly off to her room.

Bridget's father shook his head. "I don't know. We like her. And we like having her here."

"She's just in the way!" Aunt Ruth snorted. "Face it, Parker. *She's old.*"

"Well, it's up to her," Bridget's father sighed.

Bridget didn't know what the adults were talking about...until Andrew told her.

"They're putting her out because she's old and slow. She's going to a place where other old people live," he said coolly.

Andrew didn't seem to care. But Bridget did.

She ran up to her room and hugged all her
animals as tight as she could. It made her feel better.

Then, suddenly, she heard beautiful music and
saw sparkle dust all through the air. It seemed to
come straight from Bridget's mirror.

"This is very strange," Bridget thought as she
moved closer to the mirror. "What's in here? *Who's*
in here?" she said.

Suddenly a little hand came right through
the mirror!

Bridget shut her eyes quickly. When she looked
again, two hands stuck out from her mirror!

Bridget backed away, hardly believing what she
saw next…a little face between the two hands.
Then, out of the mirror stepped the cutest little
person she had ever seen.

Bridget fell right over backward.

"I didn't mean to scare you," said the person. "I'm Huggins. And you're Bridget. I know. We've been watching you."

"We?" Bridget asked carefully. "You mean there are more of you?"

"Sure! There's a whole Hugga Bunch in Huggaland...right through your mirror. I came out because you've got trouble. Maybe I can help."

Now Bridget's face brightened. "My Grandma needs help. She needs something to make her young so she can stay here with us."

Huggins chuckled. "All your Grandma needs is plenty of affection and lots of hugs."

Bridget frowned again. "No! That's just not enough. Don't you know of some medicine to make her young again?"

"I don't," Huggins started, "...but the
Book Worm might! He knows everything.
Come on!"

Huggins grabbed Bridget's hand and tugged her toward the mirror. Bridget gasped.

"I can't go through there!"

"Sure you can," Huggins grinned. "It just needs a little softening. Give me a hug."

Bridget leaned down and hugged little Huggins. Huggins tested the mirror with one hand. "We need more hugs," she said. Then, as they gave each other a super-big hug, Bridget found herself tumbling right through the mirror.

She landed with the softest of landings in the softest of lands. Bright beautiful colors and soft furry things were everywhere. Bridget looked around happily.

"How did she get in here?" a tiny, tough voice asked from above.

Bridget looked up at a boy Hugga perched on a tree limb.

"Hi, Hugsy," called Huggins. "This is Bridget. I brought her here to see the Book Worm."

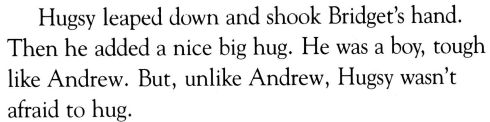

Hugsy leaped down and shook Bridget's hand. Then he added a nice big hug. He was a boy, tough like Andrew. But, unlike Andrew, Hugsy wasn't afraid to hug.

"The Book Worm, hmmm…" Hugsy thought aloud. "He's pretty far away. But I'd be happy to take you in my hugwagon."

Huggins and Bridget sat behind as Hugsy drove through this cushion-soft land. Finally they screeched to a stop near a mountainous pile of books.

The old Book Worm sat at the very top.

"We only want information," Bridget said. "Can anything make my Grandma young again?"

"Let's see…" the Book Worm said, flipping through a big book. "The aging of grandmothers may be slowed by: affection, hugging, and the knowledge that they are needed."

"But she really has to *be* young. Now! Fast!"

"Hmmm…" the Book Worm read slowly. "*Instant Youth* can be had by eating the fruit of the Youngberry Tree." He looked up. "But the only Youngberry Tree is in the Country of Shrugs!"

Huggins grabbed Hugsy in a terrified clutch.

"That's a bad place," both Huggas cried, "it's ruled by the Mad Queen of Quartz!"

Hugsy and Huggins could not let Bridget go to Shrugs all alone. So together they traveled to a hill with an old hollow tree.

"Well, this is the entrance to Shrugs," said Huggins. "Is everybody ready?"

"I...I don't care," Bridget shook out the words. "I'll do anything to save Grandma."

The three tumbled downward past slimy black roots with sticky green leaves that reached out and tried to grab them as they passed. Down...down they fell until they landed in a small forest clearing.

"Is everybody okay?" asked Bridget. They were all fine, so they started on their way. Before them was a sign, "FOLLOW THE SIDEWALK" pointing to a sidewalk standing on its side!

"Well, that's the silliest sidewalk I ever saw!" cried Bridget. "Can we walk on it?"

They all stepped carefully onto the sidewalk and found that they could walk on it, sideways!

The sideways sidewalk carried Bridget, Huggins, and Hugsy over a scary Sea of Glass, where sharp, broken pieces of glass crunched and crashed below them.

"We're scared!" cried Huggins and Hugsy, but Bridget urged them on.

"I've just got to find that Youngberry Tree," she said, "and you promised to help me!"

They all held on tightly to each other, and before too long they had passed over the Sea of Glass.

"Whew! We made it!" said Huggins, happily.

The Castle of Quartz was in sight through the trees. But, when they turned a corner, they ran right into the roaring hot breath of a terrible beast!

Bridget and Huggins shuddered in fear. But Hugsy ran straight at the beast and gave him the biggest of hugs.

In the twinkling of an eye, the "beast" became a small baby elephant.

"Uh…I've been under that awful spell for such a long time, I forgot I was an elephant," he said. "Hodgepodge is the name. Thank you for breaking the Queen's spell. I owe you one."

"Nice to meet you, Hodgepodge. Can you take us to the Youngberry Tree?" Bridget asked.

"Uhh…that's scary," Hodgepodge said slowly. "It's…uh…in the Mad Queen's garden, but as I said, I owe you one. Climb aboard!"

Bridget, Huggins and Hugsy rode on the
elephant's back through Quartz Canyon up to the
Queen's castle. They walked into the dark, cold
castle. The glistening Youngberry Tree stood before
them, laden down with beautiful golden berries. But
the tree was covered by a huge glass bell jar, hanging
from the ceiling by a golden chain!

"Omigosh! There it is!" Bridget exclaimed. "So
near and yet so far…"

No sooner had they reached the tree than a
strange and scary army of Shrugs captured the crew!
"Down on your knees!" yelled the head Shrug.
"Here comes the Queen!"
Bridget looked up in surprise. She had
expected the Mad Queen to be ugly. But she
was quite beautiful.

"Disgusting!" the Queen snapped. "Take them off to the dungeon," she said pointing to Hugsy and Huggins and Hodgepodge.

Then she turned to Bridget. "But not you," she said. "You are young and pretty, like me. I eat one Youngberry each hour so I'll stay young and beautiful. You can stay young forever, too."

"No!" Bridget yelled. "I only want the Youngberries for my Grandma…"

Suddenly, the Queen turned Bridget into a statue!

Meanwhile, Huggins and Hugsy were trying to escape from the dungeon. "Use your head," they urged Hodgepodge. "How about my trunk?" Hodgepodge asked as he wrapped it around one of the bars and gave a great yank. "We're out!" he exclaimed as the bars fell away.

They hurried through hallways and found Bridget.

Huggins broke into tears. Hugsy began to sniffle. Both of them wrapped their arms around the statue and hugged her as hard as they could.

Suddenly, hugadust landed all about Bridget and brought her back to life.

"Hurray! Now let's get out of here!" shouted Hugsy.

"Not without the Youngberries," cried Bridget who snatched up the key to the bell jar from a nearby table.

At that moment, the Queen marched in with her spoon.

"*Where's my key?*" she screamed. "I must have a Youngberry before...

But it was too late. Even as she spoke, the Queen's hands began to grow big warts and her face wrinkled up until she froze.

"Hurray!" shouted Bridget and the Huggas. "Times a-wasting. Let's go!"

Bridget and her friends unlocked the bell jar, and took a handful of Youngberries. They retraced their steps to Huggaland and raced toward the mirror.

But as Bridget stepped through the mirror, the worst thing happened. She tripped. The Youngberries fell to the floor, and all were ruined.

Just then her mother called out, "Come children, say goodbye to Grandmother."

Sadly, Bridget joined her family at the door. Even Andrew looked upset.

Bridget knew that this was their last chance. "We must try it!" she thought.

"Andrew!" she whispered. "Please! Show Grandma how much you care!"

With that, Andrew plunged forward and released all the hugs he had held inside him. "We need you!" he cried, as Bridget joined in.

Their father turned to Aunt Ruth.

"Drop those bags!" Then he began hugging Grandma too. "This family will never be too busy for each other."

Bridget smiled. "Or too busy for hugs...ever again."